Dog's eyes widened. "A contest!"

Cat's ears perked up over his magazine. "TV?" he said, his eyes glazing over. "That could lead to fame. And fame could lead to fortune. . . ."

"Cat, what are you talking about?" asked Dog.

"Don't you see, Dog?" replied Cat. "If we enter, this could be our meal ticket to the high life!"

"I thought it was just a cooking contest," said a confused Dog. "Besides, I don't know anything about cooking," he added.

Cat sighed. "Like I told you before, *anyone* can do a cooking show. Add a little of this, a little of that, and stick it in the oven. How hard can it be?"

Cookin'
with CatDog

by Annie Auerbach
illustrated by Gary Johnson

Simon Spotlight / Nickelodeon

New York   London   Toronto   Sydney   Singapore

Based on the TV series *CatDog*®
created by Peter Hannan as seen on Nickelodeon®

SIMON SPOTLIGHT
An imprint of Simon & Schuster Children's Publishing Division
1230 Avenue of the Americas, New York, New York 10020

Manufactured in the United States of America

First Edition   2 4 6 8 10 9 7 5 3 1

ISBN 0-689-83395-4

Library of Congress Catalog Card Number 00-131452

Cookin' with CatDog

Chapter One

"Hi-ho-diggety!" cheered Dog. "It's three o'clock. And you know what that means!"

"Snacktime?" Cat replied. "I could go for a nice sardine-and-sauerkraut sandwich."

"No! It's time for *Rancid's Kitchen,*" Dog answered.

"Oh no, not that horrible cooking show again," complained Cat.

Dog was quick to defend his hero. "Rancid Rabbit is the greatest chef on public access TV! Just last week he made chewy meatloaf out of a week-old pork chop. It was amazing, Cat."

Cat rolled his eyes. "Yeah, sure it was," he said sarcastically. "I'm sorry I missed it."

Dog grabbed his remote control and turned on the TV just in time.

"Well, hello to all of you wanna-be chefs out there," began Chef Rancid.

"He is so stuck-up," Cat interrupted. "He thinks he's the greatest thing since sliced bread."

"Shhh!" Dog urged.

"He's just a big rabbit in chef's clothing," said Cat. "Anyone can do a cooking show."

"Shhh!" Dog repeated. "I can't hear what Chef Rancid is saying."

"Today, we're going to make a special treat, perfect for a quick dinner or a late-night snack," Rancid continued. "Your mouths will be watering as I make one of my favorites—Rancid's Rancid Sausages."

"Yummy!" Dog shouted.

Cat felt sick at the thought of those

sausages. He went back to reading his current issue of *Fish of the Month*.

A few minutes later, Rancid made an announcement that changed the face of television forever. "To thank all of the little people out there who watch my show," Rancid began, "I'd like to announce a culinary contest happening this Friday."

Dog's eyes widened. "A contest!"

Rancid continued. "Whoever comes up with the most inventive way to use chocolate mousse, gets their very own, one-time, television cooking show."

Cat's ears perked up over his magazine. "TV?" he said, his eyes glazing over. "That could lead to fame. And fame could lead to fortune. . . ."

"Cat, what are you talking about?" asked Dog.

"Don't you see, Dog?" replied Cat. "If

we enter, this could be our meal ticket to the high life!"

"I thought it was just a cooking contest," said a confused Dog. "Besides, I don't know anything about cooking," he added.

Cat sighed. "Like I told you before, *anyone* can do a cooking show. Add a little of this, a little of that, and stick it in the oven. How hard can it be?"

Dog scratched his head. "But the show is for one time only."

"Well, my Dog, you've come to the right Cat. That's where my clever plan comes in!" Cat added excitedly. "We'll have no problem winning the contest. Then we'll become so famous on our one show, that they'll want to keep us on TV for good!"

"Gee, Cat, I don't want to *cook* for the rest of my life," said Dog. "I'd rather just *eat*."

Cat was seeing dollar signs. "When we're famous, we'll be so rich that we'll *hire* a chef so we'll never have to cook again!" he explained.

"Well . . . maybe," said Dog hesitantly. "I just don't see the fun in cooking for other people. It'd make me awfully hungry."

Cat knew he had to pull out all the stops to convince Dog. "You know, Dog," said Cat, "we only *show* the viewers how to cook. After we cook each meal on TV, we get to *eat* each meal!"

That was all Dog needed to hear. "Let's get cooking!" he called as he flew into the kitchen with a grinning Cat following right behind.

Chapter Two

Cat knew that they had to come up with something very inventive to win the contest. Believing that bigger is always better, he came up with an idea to make the tallest chocolate mousse ever.

"What do we do first?" Dog asked.

"Ah, Dog," said Cat. "What you need is a teacher, a guide, a guru . . . in a word: ME."

"But you don't know how to cook either," Dog pointed out.

"Details, details," replied Cat. "Leave that brain work to me."

"And leave the tasting to me!" Dog added.

Cat pulled out the one cookbook he owned. It was a gift from Winslow when CatDog moved in. Cat opened to the dessert section of *Cooking for Idiots: How to Cook without Burning Down the House*.

"Okay, Dog, the mousse recipe says that we need four egg yolks," Cat read aloud from the cookbook. "But since we're making a chocolate skyscraper here, we should put in more. How does forty sound?"

"Sure," answered Dog. From the refrigerator, he tossed one egg after another over his shoulder and Cat caught them in a huge pot. He stirred them together—eggshells and all.

Cat continued to read from the recipe. "Next we're going to need a quarter cup of sugar."

"How much is a quarter cup?" asked Dog, dragging out an enormous sugar sack.

"Who cares?" Cat replied. "Just put it all in. Remember we want this to be *big*. We want to win!" He looked down at the recipe as Dog went back over to the cabinet. "Dog, grab the chocolate chips."

There was no answer.

"Dog?" repeated Cat. "Doooog?"

"Uh, I couldn't find the chocolate chips," said Dog hesitantly.

"Is that because they are all over your face?" suggested Cat.

"Sorry, Cat, I couldn't help myself. I just had to have a taste." Dog told him. "How about these chocolate bars instead? They're leftover from Halloween. There must be four hundred here."

Cat looked puzzled. "You told me we ran out of candy last Halloween," he said to Dog.

"I just couldn't part with all of it," Dog said, embarrassed.

Cat shrugged. "Okay, put 'em all in."

With seven gallons of whipping cream as the final ingredient, they were all set. To stir, Cat held on to a big wooden spoon in the center of the huge pot while Dog ran around the outside of the pot.

Finally, after thirteen hours, seven minutes, and thirty-six seconds of stirring, they were finally ready to cook their creation! But the pot was way too large to fit on the stove.

Suddenly Cat had a bright idea. They would heat the outside of the pot with blowtorches.

"Gee, I didn't know cooking was so much fun!" Dog shouted from behind his safety mask.

Of course they had a few close calls. Dog nearly set the table, chairs, and even Cat on fire.

When the mixture was just the right temperature, they poured it into a huge glass bowl. It reached all the way to the ceiling.

"It's a masterpiece!" exclaimed Cat. "Now we just need to chill it so it becomes solid." But it wouldn't fit in the refrigerator.

"We could eat it instead," suggested Dog.

"Not a chance!" Cat replied. Then Cat had another idea. He shut all the windows in the house and turned on the air conditioning full blast. For two full days, CatDog was forced to walk around inside wearing scarves and ear muffs.

"It'll all be worth it when we win," Cat told Dog forty-eight hours later through chattering teeth.

Chapter Three

Friday arrived and CatDog couldn't wait to show off their enormous chocolate mousse. They got on their bike and headed to the television studio.

"Now pedal very slowly," Cat warned Dog. "This mousse is going to be hard to keep steady."

"Okay, Cat," replied Dog.

"And no chasing any garbage trucks on the way," Cat added.

Dog sighed. "Yes, Cat."

After a surprisingly smooth ride, CatDog arrived at the studio.

"So far, so good," said Cat. "Now let's go and win this contest!"

They headed inside and their excitement quickly vanished.

"Well, well, well, if it ain't the two-headed weirdo," said a voice.

It was Cliff, the leader of the Greasers.

"Hey, is dat a mousse or your new home?" joked Shriek.

"Heh . . . mousse . . . dat's funny," added Lube. He was holding a lopsided mousse in the shape of a dog collar.

"Oh, great," sighed Cat. "They're in the contest too." Then Cat took a deep breath. He was determined not to let the Greasers bother him. "Only a real cook could make a masterpiece like our mousse," Cat boasted.

"Hey! Who you callin' a crook?" Cliff growled.

And before CatDog knew it, Cliff lunged for Cat and the mousse went flying up in the air. Then it came down—all over CatDog!

"Yum!" cried Dog. "Chocolatey!"

But Cat was furious. "Our mousse is ruined!" he wailed.

Just then, Chef Rancid Rabbit walked by. He couldn't help but notice this enormous brown creature in the hallway. "Leaping lumbago!" he exclaimed. "It's a moose!"

"No, it's a CatDog," corrected Dog.

"Well, wearing mousse to look like a moose is the best use of mousse I've ever seen!" Rancid said.

Cat tried to play it cool. "Why thank you," he said to Rancid. "I, uh, I mean we worked hard on it. The moose is such a wonderful animal."

"And the dessert is even better," added Dog, licking his lips.

"Well, no need for this contest to go any further," said Rancid. "You are the winners! You get to host your own live cooking show!"

"Hi-ho-diggety!" Dog shouted.

"You can say that again!" Cat added, smiling slyly at the Greasers.

"Hi-ho-diggety!" cried Dog.

Chapter Four

CatDog had only one weekend to prepare for their television special.

Dog was worried about cooking in front of millions of people.

Cat, on the other hand, was confident. "First things first. Come with me."

Cat led Dog into town to buy proper chef's hats and uniforms. "Now at least we *look* like chefs," he told Dog.

Next, Cat bought every cookbook ever published. Back at home, Cat learned how to mince, mash, and marinate. He steamed, seasoned, and skewered. There was nothing he couldn't dice, slice, or spice.

Dog, on the other hand, thought it would be helpful if he sampled everything in the refrigerator. He became an expert on pork chops, lamb chops, and veal chops.

"Dog," pleaded Cat, "you must read some of these cookbooks. We are going to be on *live* TV. We have to look like we know what we're doing."

"Ih knopwo whyat Ih'm shoing," replied Dog with his mouth full of food.

"Fine," said Cat. "I guess I'll just have to be the brains of the operation again."

Before they knew it, it was Monday morning, the day of the big live show. Cat and Dog put on their brand-new chef's hats and uniforms.

"C'mon, Dog. Fame and fortune await!" called Cat as they headed out the door.

The television studio was buzzing with activity. Everyone was running around getting things prepared.

"Gee, DogCat, I almost didn't recognize you without the mousse," said Rancid Rabbit, barely shaking their paws.

"That's CatDog," corrected Cat.

"Right, whatever," Rancid said. "Now, your little show is going to take place over here," he continued as he lead them to the cooking area.

"Oh, boy, Cat!" said Dog. "Look at all that raw meat."

"Easy, Dog," warned Cat. "We need that for the show."

"Do you have any advice for us?" Dog asked Rancid.

"Just don't mess up or embarrass me," replied Rancid. "Maybe one or two of my viewers will tune in to see your little show," he sneered. "It'll be over soon enough." Then he sauntered away.

"That Rancid Rabbit is so stuck-up," Cat said. "Just wait until he sees what CatDog can do!"

But secretly, Dog was a little nervous. He tried to talk to his brother, but Cat was too busy getting his makeup put on.

Before long, it was show time.

"In five, four, three, two . . ." called the director as the cameras rolled.

"Welcome to *Cookin' with CatDog*," began Cat. "We're going to be preparing a savory meal and dessert that's perfect for impressing your friends and tempting your enemies."

"Today we're going to be cooking one of my favorite meat dishes," said Dog.

"*Any* meat dish is a favorite meat dish for you, Dog," joked Cat. He added a pretend laugh and mugged to the camera.

Dog gave Cat a sideways glance. He didn't think Cat's joke was very funny. Then he continued, "We're going to start by making a delicious, rare steak with a bacon grease sauce."

"That's right," added Cat. "First we must season it with a teaspoon of salt, one half teaspoon of pepper, and some chopped garlic. Set the oven to broil, and put in the steak for no longer than eight minutes," Cat instructed. All of his homework was coming in handy. "Okay, Dog, please put the steak in the oven. Dog? Dog?"

Cat turned to see what was the matter with Dog. Dog was in a daze. The smell of the raw meat was almost too much for him. Cat quickly grabbed the pan out of Dog's hands just before he gobbled up the steak. "What are you doing?" Cat whispered, glaring at Dog. Then he smiled at the camera. "This needs to go in the oven."

Dog gulped. "It just looked so juicy and smelled so good."

"Just watch the clock! And *try* to control yourself!" Cat commanded as he turned the oven as high as it would go. Then he remembered that he was on live television. "Ahem," he said, clearing his throat and smiling sweetly. "While the steak is cooking, let's move on to the potatoes."

"While most chefs would tell you to use fresh potatoes to make French fries," said Cat, "we prefer the store-bought brand."

"Yeah, and they're not too bad frozen, either," agreed Dog as he shoveled a bunch in his mouth.

"Dog, please try to control yourself,"

Cat said politely as he reached for the bag of fries. "Now give me those fries."

"No, Cat," said Dog. "I can do this part."

"Give me those fries," Cat demanded.

"No!" yelled Dog.

Cat grabbed the bag. Dog grabbed it back. Then the bag tore apart and fries flew everywhere.

"See what you did!" Cat yelled.

"It wasn't my fault!" Dog answered, vacuuming up the fries with his mouth.

"Hey, what's that smell?" Cat exclaimed. He turned and saw smoke coming from the oven. Cat grabbed an oven mitt and pulled out the smoking pan. Black smoke was everywhere! Their rare steak was now beef jerky!

Cat gave a nervous laugh. "Dog, see what happens when you cook something too long?"

Dog's eyes widened. "It looks just perfect to me! Bone appetite!"

"I think the correct French pronunciation is *bon appétit*," Cat said with an accent.

"Not for this T-bone!" Dog said as he took a huge bite.

Cat glanced over at Rancid who looked extremely angry. "Let's skip right to dessert," Cat said nervously into the camera. "It's a tasty whitefish custard in a fish-shaped graham cracker crust."

Once Cat had assembled all the necessary ingredients in a bowl, he gave it to Dog to put in the blender. But Dog hadn't paid attention during Cat's cooking lectures. Forgetting to put on the lid, he turned on the blender. The goopy mixture went everywhere!

"Dooooooooogggggg!" Cat yelled.

"Uh-oh," Dog said meekly.

"Turn it off!" Cat cried. "Turn it off!"

"I'm trying! I'm trying!" Dog replied. Finally, Dog found the off switch. By this time, however, everyone and everything was covered in smelly whitefish custard.

"Eww! Yuck!" screamed the television crew.

During all the commotion, Rancid was tearing his hair out. He was worried that this foolish CatDog would ruin his reputation for good. He ordered the director to go to a commercial.

"You're fired!" Rancid screamed at CatDog. "Get out! Just get out!"

CatDog tried to explain but they were immediately escorted out by five security guards.

"Well, Dog, you can kiss our fame and fortune good-bye," Cat said sadly.

"What about the beef jerky?" Dog asked as they headed home. "You said we could eat the food afterward. I'm hungry."

Cat just sighed and shook his head.

Chapter Five

The phone rang early the next morning. Dog answered it.

"Is this CatDog?" asked the voice on the other end.

"Yes," replied Dog. "Who is this?"

"My name is Mr. Crumb," the voice said, "and I'm calling from the public TV station."

"Cat!" Dog whispered. "It's the TV station!"

Cat grabbed the phone. "Uh-huh, uh-huh, I see, uh-huh, well, thank you very much." He hung up.

"Well?" said Dog eagerly.

Cat grinned. He couldn't believe

his ears. "My plan worked after all!" he cried. "Hundreds of viewers called the station and they want us to have our own daily cooking show!"

"Wow, wow, wow!" cheered Dog. "You're the smartest genius the world has ever known!"

"Yes, I know," replied Cat. "Now let's get down to the studio. We've got to get cooking!"

Cat couldn't have been more thrilled. "This is our second big chance, Dog. Now don't mess anything up!"

"I'll follow your lead this time!" Dog promised.

With no time to prepare, CatDog were forced to go on live TV that very afternoon.

"Hello all of you chefs out there," Cat greeted the audience. "We're so happy to be back on television. Today we're going to make a delicious halibut fillet with a side of—"

"I thought we were going to make Moldy Meat Surprise," Dog interrupted.

"Now, now, Dog," Cat replied. "I think *my* viewers would much rather learn how to make a delicacy like halibut than that poor excuse for a meal you want to make."

"They are *my* viewers, too!" Dog countered.

"Who would want to eat your moldy meat dish over my savory fish dish?" Cat sneered.

Dog stood firm. "I'm sure there are plenty of moldy meat lovers out there."

This kind of arguing continued for at least twenty-five minutes. Finally, they heard the closing music and the credits began to roll.

"I can't believe you wouldn't let me make my fish dish," said Cat.

"Well, meat is just as good as fish," replied Dog.

CatDog continued to argue all the way home.

During the taping of the next show, CatDog began to argue again. It was right after they had finished making lasagna.

"Can we eat it yet?" Dog asked. "Huh, Cat? Can we?"

"Not yet," replied Cat.

"But I'm hungry!" Dog said.

Cat tried to ignore him. "Now the best thing to do is let the lasagna cool down a little before serving," he said into the camera.

Dog was starving. While Cat wasn't looking, he took a bite of the lasagna. It *was* pretty hot, but Dog didn't care.

Cat turned and asked Dog to hand him the sour cream. Embarrassed, Dog immediately stopped chewing. When Cat turned away again, Dog took another bite. Then he stopped chewing again when Cat asked him for the sour cream. Each time Cat wasn't looking, Dog took another bite.

The audience went crazy. They knew Cat was going to blow his top. Suddenly, in the middle of a sentence, Cat let out an enormous, stinky, spicy burp! That's when he turned to see that Dog had eaten the entire lasagna!

Cat's temper exploded. He and Dog

argued and argued and argued. And the viewers loved it and loved it and loved it! They had never seen anything so funny on TV!

Chapter Six

The show was a huge hit! Suddenly, everywhere you looked there were *Cookin' with CatDog* mugs, keychains, and T-shirts. CatDog gave autographs, posed for photo shoots, and even went on talk shows. Their faces were on the cover of every magazine in town. Everyone in Nearburg knew who CatDog was.

They took limousines wherever they went. Cat loved all the attention. Dog couldn't believe all the autographs he had to give. Cat, of course, had been waiting all of his nine lives for this moment. "No pushing," said Cat. "You'll all get a turn to see your favorite stars. We love our fans."

In response to the overwhelming success, the show began to change. For starters, there was never an empty seat in the audience. Lines to get in to a taping stretched around the block and down the street.

Live, on-air phone calls were added. Sometimes the caller would be defending Cat and sometimes they would be defending Dog. The phone lines were always lit up.

Cat suggested that they add special guests. But his plan backfired when Winslow came on the show. He was supposed to demonstrate how to make chili, but ended up stirring up a little trouble of his own.

Right in the middle of the show, Winslow grabbed an orange and threw it. "Hey, Dog," he called. "Fetch!"

Never one to resist a good chase, Dog took off after the ball.

"No, Dog, no!" Cat yelled as he was dragged away from the sushi he was trying to prepare.

"Heh, heh," laughed Winslow. "Works every time."

While CatDog was busy chasing the orange around the studio audience, Winslow took the opportunity to give his own tips on cooking. But he was soon overpowered by CatDog's bickering.

"How could you play fetch in the middle of our show?" Cat scolded as they came back to the kitchen.

"I couldn't help myself," Dog replied.

"Thanks a lot, ratboy!" Cat yelled at Winslow. Then he turned to Dog and asked, "Can't you exercise a little self-control like me?"

"But it wasn't my fault," Dog protested.

"It wasn't even a ball," said Cat. "It was an orange!"

"Whatever it is, it's yummy," replied Dog.

Suddenly there was wild cheering and clapping from the audience. They loved it when CatDog argued!

The shows continued to heat up. During each show, Cat and Dog argued over what to make, how to make it, and when to eat it. Dog was always eating the meals before they were finished. Cat was always scolding Dog. Cat wanted to do an entire show about fish. Dog wanted to do an entire show on how to make a four course dinner from garbage scraps. And they always argued over who was the better chef.

Worst of all, not only were Cat and Dog fighting on live TV, they were angry at each other all the time at home when they weren't in front of a camera.

Finally, it was time for the big ratings week. CatDog knew they needed to do something spectacular to stay number one.

Cat knew how important the ratings were. "How about a cook-off?" he suggested. "We could compete against each other to see who really is the better chef once and for all."

Dog looked at his brother. He liked the idea of making anything he wanted, whether Cat liked it or not. "Sure, why not?" he told Cat.

"Then a CatDog Cook-Off it is!" Cat declared. "Just be prepared to lose, my canine friend."

"We'll see, you . . . you . . . Cat, you!" answered Dog, crossing his arms.

For the rest of the week, Cat and Dog

kept to themselves—well, as much as possible. Each thought the other was spying on them. Each was convinced the other was trying to ruin his secret recipe. By the time the big day came, Cat and Dog were enemies—enemies in chef hats having to share the same kitchen.

Chapter Seven

The big CatDog Cook-Off was the most publicized event of the year. No one knew what dishes Cat or Dog was going to make. But no one cared. Everyone just hoped that the arguments and mess-ups would be better than ever before.

"In five, four, three, two . . ." called the director as the cameras rolled.

"Hello, everyone," began Cat. "Welcome to the first, annual CatDog Cook-Off."

Dog interrupted. "I will be making a dee-licious spicy, mildewy meat enchilada with refried beans. And for dessert—"

"How do Grilled Fishheads à la Cat

sound?" Cat broke in. "They are covered in a creamy tomato sauce. And for dessert, I'll be making salmon pudding with whipped cream. It's the perfect meal."

Dog narrowed his eyes. "We'll just have to let the audience decide!" he declared.

"Well, if we must," replied Cat. "But you might as well prepare yourself now, Dog. You're going to lose."

"Will not!" Dog protested.

"Will too!" said Cat.

"Will not!" said Dog.

"Will too!" said Cat.

"Not!" said Dog.

"Too!" said Cat.

The audience went wild. The battle of the chefs was on!

As Cat and Dog each prepared their main dish, they went out of their way to make it difficult for the other one. Dog was always in Cat's way. Cat wouldn't let Dog finish a sentence without interrupting.

At one point, Cat used up all the tomatoes, so Dog was forced to use extra spicy hot sauce instead.

But Dog got his revenge when he ate one of his spicy enchiladas. The audience knew what was coming. Within a few minutes, Cat's eyes turned red and he actually breathed fire!

Once Cat cooled down, he turned to Dog and calmly said, "You want to play rough, Dog? I can play rough!" Cat grabbed an apple pie and threw it in Dog's face.

"Mmm!" said Dog, licking the apple filling off his face.

That only made Cat angrier. Cat picked up everything he could find in the kitchen and threw it at Dog. But

when it came to food, Dog was always ready. He caught almost everything in his mouth! For ammunition, Cat had to grab the one thing that he knew Dog wouldn't eat—fish sticks! In retaliation, Dog "accidentally" tossed a bag of flour in Cat's direction. Cat was covered in white from head to paw.

It was chaos! Food was flying everywhere. There was smoke coming out of the oven. The electric mixer was churning whipped cream across the room. Pots were boiling over—and so were CatDog!

"You don't know the first thing about cooking!" yelled Cat.

"You don't know the first thing about eating!" yelled Dog.

"This is war!" Cat shouted.

The audience was on its feet. Half of them were rooting for Cat, and half of them

were rooting for Dog. They even started fighting with each other!

"Cat is a better chef!" someone yelled.

"Are you crazy?" screamed someone else. "There's no one that knows his way around food like Dog!"

Dog was about to squirt Cat with seltzer water, when he suddenly stopped and turned toward the audience.

"What's the matter? Are you finally giving up?" Cat sneered, following Dog's gaze.

The audience had gotten out of control. People were screaming at each other. In fact, the TV cameras started to record the audience instead of CatDog.

Cat and Dog looked back at each other and smiled. Then they started to giggle. Then they started to laugh really hard. In fact, they couldn't remember the last time they had laughed so hard.

"I'm sorry I've been so horrible, Cat," said Dog.

"I'm sorry you've been so horrible too," replied Cat.

CatDog hugged, wiping tears from their eyes.

"Come on," began Cat. "Let's finish this cook-off *together*."

"Yeah," agreed Dog. "We can still make something for dessert."

"If we can *find* something," joked Cat.

So CatDog turned off the oven, stopped the pots from boiling over, and worked together to make a mud pie from what they could salvage of the ingredients.

"Would you hand me the butter?" Cat asked politely.

"Sure," answered Dog. "Could you please pass the ice cream?"

"Of course, Dog," replied Cat. "Just be

careful. It's a little cold."

"You are so thoughtful," said Dog with a smile.

The audience stopped fighting with each other and turned to stare at CatDog.

Suddenly there was an on-air phone call.

"Hello, and welcome to *Cookin' with CatDog*," said Cat. "What can we help you with today?"

"WHAT'S WRONG WITH YOU TWO?" screamed the voice on the other end. "Where is the yelling CatDog that I tune in to watch?!"

"YEAH!" screamed someone from the studio audience. "You can't be nice to each other. That's boring!"

"You stink!" yelled someone else.

"So does your kitchen!" came another voice.

And before CatDog knew it, the entire audience was booing and hissing. "Be mean to each other! Throw a pie! Throw a toaster! Throw anything!" they yelled.

CatDog looked at each other. They hated being mean to each other over the last few weeks. It was exhausting! CatDog looked back at the audience, who was now becoming angrier and angrier.

"Dog," said Cat quietly.

"Yeah?" Dog whispered back.

"I think we'd better get out of here before *we* get cooked!" whispered Cat. And with that they both ran out of the studio and straight home.

A few days later, Dog was once again watching a TV show on the public access channel. It was *15 Minutes of Fame Musical Acts*.

Rancid Rabbit was the host. To make up for the CatDog cooking disaster, the network had given Rancid three new TV shows in their prime-time lineup.

"This show stinks, Dog. I can't believe you can watch this garbage." Cat complained.

"I love this show, Cat, but this band will never win the contest," Dog said, pointing to the band on TV.

Then Rancid announced that the weekly contest awarded the winning band $15,000 cash.

Suddenly Cat had another idea . . .

Hi-ho-diggety! Here's a sneak peek at chapter book #8.

The Most World Records

Rancid cleared his throat and said, "Now, I'd like to welcome all of you to Nearburg's first annual Most World Records Contest. The team with the most world records will not only take home some million-dollar prizes, but will also go down in history."

Cat wasn't listening to the mayor's speech. He was looking around at the other teams, sizing up the competition. There were three other teams: the Greasers, Eddie the Squirrel and some of his pals, and Mervis and Dunglap. "Well, Mervis and

Dunglap are useless. I don't have to worry about them," Cat thought to himself. "But where is that Winslow? I'm not giving him eight-and-half percent for nothing."

". . . and so, in my opinion, being a good sport is overrated," Mayor Rancid continued. "It's all about winning—winning with a capital W."

"Yeah!" the crowd cheered.

"Losers are just that, losers!" Rancid declared. "Whoever said, 'It's not about winning or losing, it's how you play the game' must have been a loser!"

"Yeah! Loser!" the crowd cheered.

"Like CatDog!" added Cliff.

"Yeah!" the crowd cheered.

"Ha!" Cat shouted. "You'll all see! Victory will be mine! Uh . . . I mean ours!"

"Yeah!" Dog yelled in support.